The Three Little Brown Piggies

Published by UMI (Urban Ministries, Inc.)
Chicago, Illinois
Text and illustrations copyright © 2006 by UMI (Urban Ministries, Inc.)

Library of Congress Control Number: 2006907099
Hardcover Library of Congress Control Number: 2006936865

ISBN 10: 1-932715-83-5
Hardcover ISBN 10: 1-934056-21-9
ISBN 13: 978-1-932715-83-5
Hardcover ISBN 13: 978-1-934056-21-9

Produced by Color-Bridge Books, LLC
Printed in the U.S.A.

THE THREE LITTLE BROWN PIGGIES

Retold and Illustrated by
Fred Crump, Jr.

Urban Ministries, Inc.

ot long ago, in a little town called Piggyville, there lived a mother pig and her three sons. They were named Pokey, Punky, and Picky.

One day Mother Pig told her three little brown piggies that they were old enough to leave home to seek their fortunes. She gave them each a small gold coin and waved bye-bye.

"Watch out for the Big Bad Wolf!" she called as they skipped down the path. "His favorite dinner is Piggy Potpie."

Off To Seek Their Fortunes

efore long they met a farmer with a load of straw. Pokey said, "A nice soft straw house would be fun to live in." So he bought the straw and decided to take a nap on it before going to work on his new home.

Next Punky and Picky met a woodcutter with a load of twigs. Punky said, "A twig house would let the cool breezes blow in." So he bought the twigs and decided to compose a song on his guitar to celebrate having a new home (which he had not yet built).

Picky went on alone and soon met a mason with a load of bricks. "A brick house would last forever," he said. And he bought the bricks and some cement and went to work at once.

Straw, Twigs, and Bricks

So Pokey built a sloppy-floppy little straw house and spent his days "goofing off." And Punky built a rickety-wobbly little twig house and spent his days twanging on his guitar.

And every day the two brothers went to laugh at Picky, who was working very hard to build a fine, strong brick house.

Picky tried to warn them. "Remember the Big Bad Wolf, brothers dear," he said. "He might tear down your houses."

"Ha-ha!" They just laughed.

"There is no Big Bad Wolf," said Pokey. "Mama just made that up to keep us from having too much fun."

"I see it didn't work," said Picky with a frown.

ow one day Big Bad Weevil Wolf was busy in his kitchen. "Today I am in the mood for Piggy Potpie!" he said as he chuckled. He put on a big kettle of water to boil and pulled out his recipe book.

"Hm-m-m, let's see," he hummed happily, "we have the three big potatoes, and three long golden carrots, and three purple turnips, and three golden onions, and three cups of hot pepper, and—oh, no! We don't have three fat little piggies!"

So he put on his coat and hat and went out to find three little pigs for his Piggy Potpie.

Making Piggy Potpie

Before long Weevil Wolf saw Pokey Pig go into his little straw house. He knocked—tappity-tap—on the door.

"Who's there?" called Pokey.

"A friendly neighbor," said Weevil. "I see you are new in the neighborhood, and I'd like to invite you to dinner."

But Pokey stuck his head out the window and saw it was the Big Bad Wolf.

"Oh, no!" he squealed. "I would *be* your dinner!"

"Right!" Weevil laughed. "Now, hold on to something because I am going to blow down your flimsy straw house."

An Invitation To Dinner

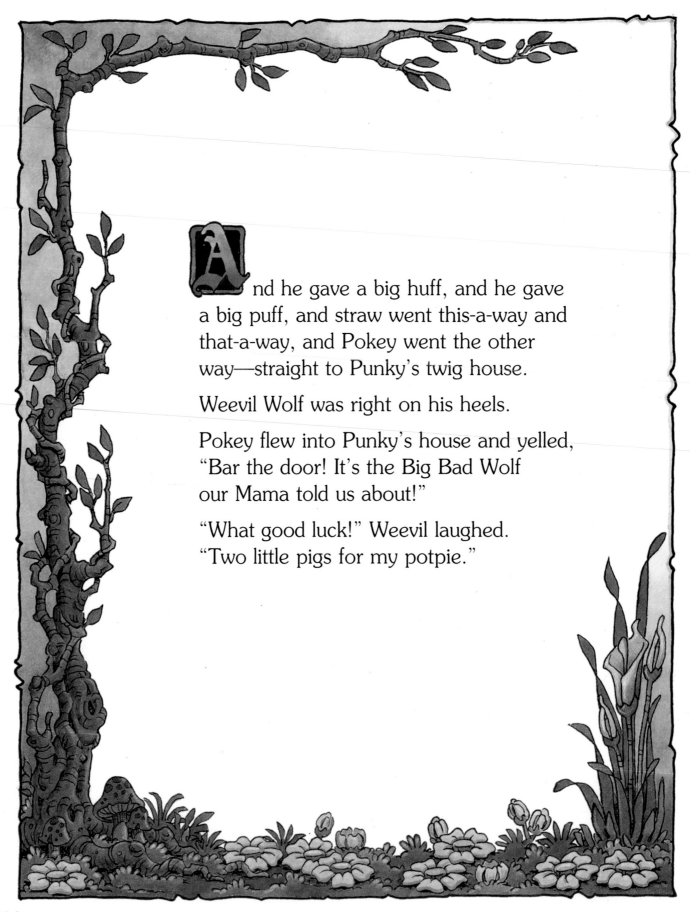

And he gave a big huff, and he gave a big puff, and straw went this-a-way and that-a-way, and Pokey went the other way—straight to Punky's twig house.

Weevil Wolf was right on his heels.

Pokey flew into Punky's house and yelled, "Bar the door! It's the Big Bad Wolf our Mama told us about!"

"What good luck!" Weevil laughed. "Two little pigs for my potpie."

Weevil Huffed and Puffed

hen he knocked—tappity-tap-tap—
on Punky's twig door.

"Who . . . who . . . who is there?"
squeaked Punky.

"I am a talent scout for Mootown Records,"
said Wicked Old Weevil, "and I want to
hear you twang on your guitar."

"Wow!" said Punky, and he threw open
the door before Pokey could stop him.
"Oh, no! You are the Big Bad Wolf!"
squealed Punky.

"And you are not too smart!" shouted
Pokey as he slammed and locked
the door.

Weevil Huffed and Puffed

Then he knocked—tappity-tap-tap—on Punky's twig door.

"Who . . . who . . . who is there?" squeaked Punky.

"I am a talent scout for Mootown Records," said Wicked Old Weevil, "and I want to hear you twang on your guitar."

"Wow!" said Punky, and he threw open the door before Pokey could stop him. "Oh, no! You are the Big Bad Wolf!" squealed Punky.

"And you are not too smart!" shouted Pokey as he slammed and locked the door.

Weevil Wolf Tricked Punky

"Here we go again!"
said Wicked Old Weevil.

Then he huffed and puffed,
and twigs went this-a-way,
and twigs went that-a-way,
and the two squealing
pigs went the other way. . . .

ACME DISGUISE ☆ KIT ☆

Punky's Twig House Collapsed

Straight to Picky Pig's strong brick house.

"Company is coming, brother dear!" they shouted as they flew through the door.

"Lock the door!
  Quick!
    Fast!
      Hurry!"

Lickety-Split To Picky's House

ow perfect," said Weevil Wolf. "Three little piggies. My Piggy Potpie recipe is now complete."

He knocked—tappity-tap-tap-tap—on Picky's door.

"Who is it?" called Picky.

"The apple peddler," said Weevil.

"Leave a basket of apples at the door and I will pay you tomorrow," said Picky.

"Drat!" hissed the wolf, and he knocked—tappity-tap—again.

"Who is it?" called Picky.

"It is the insurance man selling wolf protection policies."

"Thank you," said Picky, "but I am living in a brick insurance policy."

Weevil laughed. "I'll bet I can cancel your policy."

Then he took a big deep breath,
he huffed a big huff and puffed a
big puff, and he blew and he blew.

But nothing happened.

He huffed and puffed a bunch of times,
and he snorted and stomped around.

Finally, his eyes crossed,
  he turned blue . . .
      and he fell flat on his face.

Weevil Huffed and Puffed

ow what?" Weevil whimpered.
Then he thought of the chimney!

Up a tree,
  onto the roof,
    and down into the chimney
      went Wicked Old Weevil Wolf.

303 ELM

He Climbed Up to the Chimney

And he landed in Picky's big pot of hot turnip soup!

Weevil Wolf yelled and squealed and whooped and hollered and crawled back up the chimney a good bit faster than he had crawled down!

He ran straight home and got into bed and covered up his head and whimpered for three whole days.

Weevil Landed in the Hot Soup

As for Pokey and Punky, they went straight to the mason and bought two loads of bricks.

Now there are three little brick houses on the hill. Farmer Pokey grows beans and carrots.

Farmer Punky grows corn and tomatoes.

And Farmer Picky grows potatoes and onions.

Every Saturday the three little brown piggies sell their crops at a little roadside stand. . . .

Three Little Piggy Farmers

Their best customer is Weevil Wolf. He needs lots of vegetables for a new recipe he invented.

It is called Veggie Potpie.